I Saw Three Ships

A MAGICAL CHRISTMAS TALE BY

Elizabeth Goudge

Illustrated by Margot Tomes

DAVID R. GODINE · *Publisher*

Boston

This edition published in 2009 by
David R. Godine · *Publisher*
Post Office Box 450
Jaffrey, New Hampshire 03452
www.godine.com

LIBRARY OF CONGRESS
CATALOGING-IN-PUBLICATION DATA
Goudge, Elizabeth, 1900–
I saw three ships/Elizabeth Goudge ;
illustrated by Margot Tomes.
p.   cm.
Summary: In spite of the fact that Polly's two aunts will
not leave the door unlocked on Christmas Eve, their
cottage is still visited by three wise men, one of whom
has come home to stay after a long absence.
ISBN 978-1-56792-504-3 (softcover)
[1. Christmas--Fiction.] I. Tomes, Margot, ill.   II. Title.
PZ7.G71Is   2008
[Fic]—dc22
2008019752
FIRST SOFTCOVER PRINTING, 2013
Printed in the United States of America

I Saw Three Ships

One

"But we always did it at home," said Polly.

"My dear," said Aunt Dorcas, "at home you had a man in the house."

"But we've got The Hat in the hall," said Polly.

"My dear," said Aunt Dorcas, "it is not such an adequate protection."

Aunt Constantia said nothing, but sighed and touched her eyes with her dainty handkerchief.

This was almost always the end of their arguments. Polly said they did it at home, Aunt Dorcas said they could not do it without a man in the house, Aunt Constantia touched her eyes as a tribute to the memory of the owner of The Hat, and Polly said no more.

But Polly decided that instead of folding up her soft mouth into a pink rosette of silence, and then going off and doing the thing just the same, this time she would argue the matter out before doing it just the same.

"In the country," she said, "there is not a farm that does not leave its doors unlocked day and night during the season of Christmas. At our farm Papa and Mamma offered hospitality to all who came. By day the kitchen was full of hungry people being fed, and by night the angels went up and down the stairs."

"Go along with you!" said Constantia.

"They did," said Polly. "I heard them. Not their footsteps, for those were too light, but their feathers brushing the paneling."

"Sparrows in the roof," said Dorcas. "Now listen,

my dear. Your papa's farm was in a peaceful country district, but in a seaport town such as this a great many undesirable people are about at the holiday season; and as I keep telling you, dear child, the only masculine protection in this house is your poor dear grandfather's Hat in the hall."

Constantia applied her handkerchief to the corner of her left eye, for her father had been dead for forty years, and her elder brother and his wife had died in a road accident ten months ago. This was their little daughter's first Christmas without them. Polly was dry-eyed. She missed her father and mother and the farm but she was happy living with her two elderly aunts. They loved her and she always had her own way with them, whether they knew it or not. She intended to have it now. "The Wise Men might come," she said. "I was always expecting them at home, but they didn't come. I expect we were too far inland. They might come here. You wouldn't want to lock your door on the Wise Men, would you?"

"Don't talk nonsense, child," said Dorcas impatiently. "And there *are* no wise men. I have never met a man yet who was not foolish."

Dorcas had reason for her impatience. Her father, the doctor, though much loved in the town, had been a fine old reveler and gambler, and when he died there had been so little money left that she and Constantia had had to leave their elegant house in

Prospect Street, and come to Holly Cottage in Fish Street above the harbor. Their elder brother Roger, Polly's father, had disgraced them by going off to the country, where he had bought a farm and proceeded to indulge a hitherto unsuspected passion for pigs. Their second brother Tom, also older than themselves, had been so wild a boy that he had run off to sea at an early age and had never been heard of again. Dorcas had loved him and thought of him still with longing. Constantia scarcely remembered him, but both sisters sighed with exasperation whenever they remembered either of their brothers. In the Flowerdew family wisdom had resided only in the female branch.

"The Wise Men might come," said Polly. "Why not? Susan at the sweetshop told me that Christ Himself came to the West Country when He was a little boy."

"That's only a legend, dear," said Dorcas.

"What's a legend, Aunt?" asked Polly.

"A story whose truth cannot be proved," said Dorcas.

"You can't prove God," said Polly. "Where did they land, Aunt Constantia?"

"My love!" ejaculated Constantia in distress.

"It might have been here," said Polly. "I expect He sailed into our harbor just when the cocks were crowing. There He was, walking up and down the

streets of our town very early in the morning, and the doors were locked and no one rang the bells. Wasn't that odd?"

Her aunts looked at her, Dorcas adjusting her spectacles and Constantia pushing hers distractedly up on her forehead. Even after ten months' experience of her they did not know what to make of their niece at times. They suffered from the sensation that she was older than they were.

She sat there looking very demure in the long skirts of a hundred and sixty years ago, but her sloe-black eyes were alight in her thin heart-shaped brown face and a dimple was showing beside her mouth. Suddenly she grabbed the cat, jumped up and ran out of the room. Snatching her red cloak off the peg in the hall, she ran out of the front door into the little garden that separated the cottage from the cobbled street that led down steeply to the harbor and the sea. Peering anxiously through the draped curtains, her aunts saw her sitting on the low wall in the winter sunshine. She was singing to the cat, and the words of her song came through the tiny crack of open window that was all Dorcas allowed in the parlor even on the warmest day.

> *I saw three ships come sailing in,*
> *On Christmas day, on Christmas day;*
> *I saw three ships come sailing in,*
> *On Christmas day in the morning.*

"My dear," said Constantia to Dorcas in trembling tones, "we must shoot the top bolt tonight. She can't reach that."

"My dear," said Dorcas to Constantia, "she'd find a way to reach it. What we must do is take away the key."

> *And what was in those ships all three,*
> *On Christmas day, on Christmas day;*
> *And what was in those ships all three,*
> *On Christmas day in the morning?*

Polly was no longer sitting on the wall but dancing on the tiny scrap of lawn, holding the cat aloft and singing as she danced. She was light as thistledown on her feet and the old traditional air proved itself a perfect dancing measure. Watching the dancing child and the sparkling sunshine of this springlike Christmas Eve, the elderly ladies became dazzled and confused. Dorcas hummed the tune, nodding her head and tapping her foot, and Constantia became aware of bells and brightness, hosts of capering children and men and women clapping their hands. Before they knew what they were doing they were both singing too, and Constantia was clapping her hands.

The Virgin Mary and Christ were there,
On Christmas day, on Christmas day;
The Virgin Mary and Christ were there,
On Christmas day in the morning.

"Constantia, what *do* you think you are doing with your hands?" asked Dorcas severely.

"Your foot, Dorcas," said Constantia in mild reproof. "And did you know you were singing?"

"I was not singing," said Dorcas. "Where's that child?"

The singing had stopped and both the garden and the street were empty.

"Vanished," said Constantia.

"I told her she was to help me scour the saucepans this morning, if you remember," said Dorcas. "Upon her return she must be punished, Christmas Eve or no Christmas Eve. Supperless to bed. No, Constantia, not you; I'll go after her. The silver is on the table. Clean it, my dear."

Lifting her shabby skirts with an air, Dorcas vanished elegantly from the room to put on her cloak and bonnet. Sighing, Constantia sat down at the table before the silver . . . Dorcas always took the more exciting duties to herself.

Two

IN HER HEART Constantia sympathized with Polly's dislike of the scouring, polishing, dusting, and sweeping that was their life at Holly Cottage, and had been ever since she could remember, for since their father died they had been too poor to keep a maid. Dorcas was house-proud and had found satisfaction and fulfillment in a lifetime's devotion to her possessions, to the brass pots and pans, the silver, the china, the linen, the furniture, and the little house that held them all. But Constantia, though she never showed it, was at times madly impatient. She longed for something to happen. She thought sometimes how exciting it would be if their brother Tom should suddenly come home and upset the habits of the whole house from top to bottom. She thought now how lovely it would be if looking from her window tomorrow morning she should see three ships. . .

She polished a beautiful rattail spoon and was aware of sunshine held in the bowl. She got up, dragged the table to the window, pulled back the draped curtains, flung the window wide, and sat down again with a beating heart; for though the whole of the sunlit street was now revealed to her gaze, she was also revealed to the gaze of the sunlit street. Anyone who passed by would see her polishing the silver. What would Dorcas say, Dorcas who for forty years had kept the curtains so closely draped that no one had been able to see the Misses Flowerdew doing their own work because they were too poor to keep a maid?

. . . And now here was Constantia giving the whole show away, polishing silver at an open window, her voice raised in song as gaily as that of any gypsy woman sitting at her caravan door.

Pray, whither sailed those ships all three,
On Christmas day, on Christmas day;
Pray, whither sailed those ships all three,
On Christmas day in the morning?

She was not looking at the street as she polished a fine old silver pepper pot, warming to her task now that the sun was on her face and the fresh sea wind was stirring the silvery fair curls that escaped from her mobcap.

"Since you ask me, ma'am," said a voice. "Bethlehem."

Constantia stifled a small scream and dropped the pepper pot, and the seafaring character who was leaning his arms comfortably on the low garden wall, only a few yards from her, raised his pleasing baritone voice in song for her information.

> *O they sailed into Bethlehem,*
> *On Christmas day, on Christmas day;*
> *O they sailed into Bethlehem,*
> *On Christmas day in the morning.*

The tune got into his feet and he took his arms from the wall and began to jig. The jig might have turned into a hornpipe had not the beauty of a thin swan-like silver milk jug caught his eyes. "Now that's a pretty thing!" he ejaculated, and propped himself on the wall once more. His dark eyes sparkled. Constantia found her heart was beating fast and, hardly knowing what she did, she moved her hand and laid it on top of a valuable caddy spoon, hiding it. As she did so the sun sparkled on her mother's diamond ring, which this morning she had slipped on the fourth finger of her right hand. She had not worn it for years, but this morning, because it was Christmas Eve and because Polly had been looking in her

jewel case and admiring the pretty things she so seldom used because Dorcas disapproved of jewelry,
she had lightheartedly put it on. Just now and then,
since Polly had come, lightheartedness had visited
her occasionally for a few mad moments.

"And that's another pretty thing," murmured the

seafaring character. "Diamonds round a pearl." He hitched himself a little farther over the wall. He wore gold earrings himself and they looked well with his sun-baked, weather-beaten countenance that might have been carved out of a bit of old wood, so haphazard were his features and so deeply lined his skin. Nevertheless it was an attractive face and something about it made Constantia say to herself, "This is a wise man."

It was the earrings and the cut of his jib that had made her think he was a sailor, for he was not dressed as one. He wore a smart bottle-green coat with brass buttons and a waistcoat embroidered with crimson carnations. His cocked hat was under his arm and the sun glinted on his fine white wig. Constantia wished The Hat were in sight. What was the good of it hanging in the hall? She straightened her shoulders, lifted her hand from the caddy spoon, reached for her polishing rag, and polished it. She was game. Flight did not occur to her.

"Though you could call any town Bethlehem on Christmas Eve," said the man.

Constantia said evenly, "You mean that all over the world every town on Christmas Eve is waiting for the bells to ring in the morning?"

"Not quite all over the world, ma'am," he said. "Though I know it says so in the carol. You can't rely on carols for strict truthfulness. I've been all over the world and heard the bells but seldom. That's one reason why I've come back. Now that's a pretty thing, ma'am, that sugar bowl. Is it ivy leaves engraved on it?"

And this time he leaned so far over the wall that the strong masculine odor of beer and tobacco reached her and made her recoil. "Vine leaves," she replied faintly, and moved the bowl to the other side of the table.

He saw that he was distressing her and drew back. "Good morning, ma'am," he said, bowed to her, replaced his hat, and strolled off down the street singing as cheerfully as a blackbird.

And all the bells on earth shall ring,
On Christmas day, on Christmas day;
And all the bells on earth shall ring,
On Christmas day in the morning.

Three

POLLY, WELL AWARE that Aunt Dorcas would be soon in pursuit, raced down Fish Street, Tibby the cat still under her arm, and ran along the seawall until she reached the flight of steps that led down to the great rocks on the sands below. They were uncovered now, at low tide, and made a safe refuge from Aunt Dorcas, for the steps were so slippery with seaweed that only seamen, children, dogs, and the mad Frenchman ever attempted to go down them. Polly was down them in a trice, and picking her way over the rocks to her favorite hiding place beside the anemone pool. The sea was gold and the beautiful crimson frilled anemones were as lovely as any spring flowers. She cuddled Tibby in her arms, under her cloak, and began to sing softly, rocking Tibby to the tune.

And all the Angels in Heaven shall sing,
On Christmas day, on Christmas day;
And all the Angels in Heaven shall sing,
On Christmas day in the morning.

"Ver-r-ry unseasonable weather," said a voice. "Mademoiselle Pollee, may I stroke the small cat? Holy Mary, Mother of God, pray for us sinners."

Polly was not startled by the loud voice breaking in suddenly upon her peace, or by the mixture of subjects, for the Frenchman was a friend of hers and she was used to his sudden appearances and disappearances and his love of cats and of prayer. When he was not kneeling in the old church by the harbor, saying Popish Latin prayers at the top of his high cracked voice and telling his Popish beads to the scandal of all good Protestants going in and out to polish the brass or beat the dust

out of the hassocks, he was striding up and down the steep streets of the little town followed by all the cats of the neighborhood, who adored him not only for the fish heads he kept wrapped in newspaper in his pockets for them, but also for some quality in himself which appealed to their sense of breeding.

Polly opened her cloak and Tibby leaped from its shelter into the Frenchman's arms. Then she shifted along to make room for him to sit beside her. She was very fond of him and was quite unable to understand why people called him mad. She considered him a very wise man indeed. She was sorry for him, too, for she had heard the aunts discussing him one night and learned that he had escaped from Paris at the height of something called the Terror, after he had been told that his wife and small son had been murdered in the place of safety where he had placed them. She only vaguely understood the meaning of these things, but she was sorry, and, remembering them, now moved close to him, so that they sat companionably together looking out at the sunlit sea.

"I don't think it's unseasonable weather," said Polly. "I think it ought to be like spring at Christmas. It's nice to have a calm sea for the three ships and you want Mary and the little boy to feel warm on board, don't you?"

She wondered what she had said to make him look at her suddenly with his eyes nearly starting out of his head. "Marie and the little boy!" he ejaculated fiercely. "Ought I to have come away without seeing with my own eyes the truth of what they told me?"

Polly thought she'd better change the subject. "I'm hanging up my stocking," she announced. "I wrote down what I wanted and put the bit of paper on the kitchen mantelpiece like Aunt Constantia told me to."

He was instantly at her service. "And what do you hope to have in your stocking, mademoiselle?" he asked courteously.

Polly ticked the items off on her fingers. "A sugar mouse. A red ribbon for my hair. An apple, and three walnuts painted gold. A doll. A shell that sounds like the sea. A pincushion. A string of beads. At least I should like the beads but I don't know if I shall get them because Aunt Dorcas doesn't approve of jewelry."

"Why does your good aunt not approve of jewelry?" asked the Frenchman with a touch of indignation.

"Vanity of vanities, all is vanity," said Polly through her nose, and with such obvious and wicked mimicry that it was the Frenchman's turn to change the subject.

"Did I ever tell you about the nest of mice I put in my grandfather's best wig, mademoiselle?" he inquired. "I was not a good small boy. No. My poor grandfather, he was shortsighted, and when he clapped his wig upon his head. . ."

"Go on!" cried Polly eagerly. "Were they very small mice? Did they squeak? Did your grandfather yell?"

In a moment or two they were absorbed and happy. The sea gulls wheeled and laughed "Ha! Ha!" above them and the anemones expanded in the sun-warmed water of the rock pool like red roses in an early June.

Four

"OF ALL THE tiresome children!" said Dorcas to herself. She had already been to the sweetshop and the haberdasher's and found no Polly there, and now she was picking her way delicately along the seawall.

She gathered her old brown cloak firmly about her, as though the balmy southwest wind were a savage northeaster, and peered out from the recesses of her brown beaver bonnet like an owl from the shelter of a hollow tree. Nevertheless there was the hint of a smile upon her usually grim mouth. For though she did not admit it she was enjoying this expedition in search of the erring Polly. The sharp tang of the seaweed lying in shining coils on the sand below her was delightful. The sparkle of the sea in the sunshine raised her spirits. Turning to look at the little town, she found she had forgotten how pretty it was with its steep cobbled streets, climbing the hill, its old red roofs all higgledy-piggledy, and the plumes of smoke from the chimneys azure in the clear air. Christmas Day tomorrow. Had they everything for the child's stocking? She began to count up the items. A sugar mouse. A red hair ribbon. An apple, and three walnuts painted gold. (What absurd things children did think they wanted!) A doll. A shell that sounded like the sea. A pincushion. Yes, that was the lot. Not the beads, of course, for she'd not have it on her conscience to teach a child vanity, but to make up for that she had added of her own accord a little netted purse with sixpence in it.

Where *was* the child? She had reached the end of the harbor wall and still no sign of her. She stopped for a moment, looking up at the gulls and at three golden clouds like ships floating before the breeze. How it had brought back the past to hear Polly singing the old carol their mother had taught them when they were young. Tom had sung it best. He had had a voice like a blackbird. What had happened to him now? Her spirits, which had been

high, fell a little as a sense of time touched her. How slowly it crawled and yet how fast it flew. She had been young and now she was old and the years between had vanished as though they had never been.

A hand plucked at her cloak and a coarse voice demanded a copper for a crust of bread. She swung around indignantly, adjusting her spectacles to give old one-eyed, one-legged Rags-and-Bones a piece of her mind. Coming up behind her like that, nearly startling the life out of her! As a child in the nursery she could remember him crying "Rags-and-Bones" up and down the street. If she was getting old he must be unbelievably old. Looking at him, she found that he was. He was bald as an egg. His round button of a red nose and his one sharp bright eye looked out from a thicket of struggling white beard and whiskers. For the rest he was just rags and bones.

Had he any memories? Had he once had a voice like a blackbird's and sung of three ships? She took out her shabby old purse and gave him a copper.

"Make it two, lady," he suggested blithely.

She made it two and to her great astonishment heard herself saying, "I've known you a long time, Rags-and-Bones."

"Make it three, then," he said.

She made it three.

"Ay," he said. "We're gettin' on. I don't want to go hungry this Christmas. Nor dry neither. Might be my last."

He spoke with the utmost cheerfulness. She remembered that he had always been a cheerful soul, in spite of his one leg and his one blind eye. "How did you lose your leg and the sight of your eye, Rags-and-Bones?" she asked suddenly, and was astonished that in all the years of her life this question had never occurred to her before.

"In the wars," said Rags-and-Bones. "I was a drummer boy. But there was worse off than me an' I kept smiling."

"You learned wisdom early," said Dorcas.

"Ay," said old Rags-and-Bones, and, closing his clawlike hand on his wealth, he crawled away between two gray old cottages like a lizard escaping between two gray old stones.

Dorcas turned around and saw Polly running toward her, pink-cheeked and laughing. She straightened herself in severity, freeing her arms from her cloak as though to administer a box on the ears. "Ha! Ha!" laughed the gulls overhead. Dorcas bent down and held out her arms and Polly ran into them.

Five

Polly was not sent supperless to bed. Dorcas did not forget about the well-deserved punishment but she was feeling curiously relaxed, oddly reluctant to pursue the path of duty. "I hope I'm not sickening for something," she said to Constantia as they sat before the fire filling Polly's stocking after the child had gone upstairs.

"Do you feel feverish?" asked Constantia anxiously.

"No," said Dorcas, "but it's Wednesday and I haven't polished the furniture."

"You must be ill," said Constantia. "Have you a headache?"

"No," said Dorcas. "I never felt better in my life. How much beer can you buy with three coppers?"

Constantia bent over and felt her sister's pulse. It was perfectly steady.

"I wonder if there's anything in it," said Dorcas.

"In what, dear?" asked Constantia tenderly.

"In this idea that one must leave the door unlocked on Christmas Eve."

"I don't care if there's anything in it or not," said Constantia firmly. "I am locking both the back and front doors and taking both keys to bed with me. What's more, I am going to bed now, Dorcas, and so are you."

They plumped up the parlor cushions and swept up the hearth, latched every window firmly, and pulled all the curtains so that not a finger of moonlight could thrust itself in anywhere. They locked the parlor, dining-parlor, and kitchen doors upon the hall side so that if a thief broke a window and climbed in he would find himself unable to get farther. They wound the grandfather clock in the hall, brushed The Hat and replaced it on its peg. They bolted the back and front doors, locked them, and Constantia put the keys in her pocket. Then, carrying their lighted candle and Polly's stocking, they slowly climbed the stairs, Dorcas leading.

"Gold, Frankincense, and Myrrh," said Dorcas. "Their wealth, their prayer, their death. Three good gifts."

They left their candle on the landing and tiptoed into Polly's little room. The window was uncurtained and the moonlight streamed in showing her lying in apparent sleep, rosy and happy; but Constantia thought her eyelashes flickered. A stocking, pair to the one the aunts had already filled, hung from the foot of her bed and Tibby the cat was asleep in the crook of her arm. The aunts exchanged the empty stocking for the full one, looked lovingly at the child for a moment, and then with one accord turned to the open window. It had a view that tonight was unusually lovely. Below them the slanting roofs of the little town fell steeply to the harbor, and to a sea so calm that the moon had made a golden pathway upon it. The stars shone so brightly that they made a weight of glory in the sky. It was so quiet that the murmur of the sea came up to them almost as clearly as though they stood on the shore. The pathway of gold seemed waiting for something.

"It's so warm tonight," said Constantia. "And this window is so high up. Need we shut it?"

"Not this one," said Dorcas. "Nor curtain it. Then in the morning, Constantia, she will see the ships."

"Come along to your bed at once, Dorcas," said Constantia, and led her sister firmly from the room.

As soon as they had gone Polly opened her eyes, sat up, and looked appreciatively at the bulging stocking. Moving carefully, not to disturb Tibby, she wriggled down to the bottom of the bed. To open her stocking before the morning would not be playing fair, but she could feel it and see if her requirements had been met. She counted carefully. The doll. The mouse. The apple and walnuts. The shell. The

hair ribbon, perhaps, but owing to the small space it took up she could not be sure. The pincushion. Something she did not know about, but which was not beads. There were no beads. Even though she had been sure there would be no beads she felt a pang of disappointment, for she had wanted them more than anything else. Well, never mind, the sugar mouse was there, and right on top too, and she licked his nose for comfort. Then she crept back inside her nice warm bed and waited. When there had been silence for some while she got out of bed, put on her scarlet dressing gown, crept downstairs, and lit the two silver candlesticks that stood on the hall table beneath The Hat. For a moment or two it was disconcerting to find the front door locked and the key gone, and the back door the same, but Polly was not a child to be disconcerted for long. Unlocking the parlor door, she went in, drew back the curtains, unlatched the window, and opened it wide. But she did not go back to bed again.

She curled up in a corner of the sofa and lay there looking out the window. So brilliant was the full moon that she could see the holly berries on the tree in the garden, and behind the little tree the whitewashed walls of the cottages opposite gleamed like snow. Lamplit windows shone orange and gold in the snowy walls and up above them the irregular old roofs and chimneys cut strange shapes out of the luminous sky. At first she heard footsteps passing up and down the street, and people calling out greetings, and she heard the church clock strike ten times, each note lovely as a falling star. Then there were no more footsteps and the bright squares of gold and orange faded one by one from the moonlit walls.

She did perhaps doze a little at last, for she heard no footsteps and did not see him come. Lifting heavy lids, she saw him standing motionless across the way, leaning against the white wall, very tall, wrapped in a dark cloak but with silver about his head to tell her he had come from heaven . . . Gabriel . . . and the door had been locked against him!

She was not in the least frightened, for though she had never seen him before, had she not heard his wings brushing against the paneling at home? But she did hesitate at the window, for she did not know how to address him. How did one address an archangel?

"Sir!" she called at last. "Sir!"

He came across at once, opened the gate noiselessly, crossed the little lawn and leaned his arms on the windowsill. She saw now that he was not an angel at all but a tall man with a brown face, quite old, even older than the aunts. What she had thought was a halo was an exceptionally beautiful white wig. If she was disappointed it was only for the moment.

"Are you a Wise Man?" she asked.

"That depends what you mean by wise," he said. "I've learned a great deal. Sprite, have you a name?"

"Polly Flowerdew," she said.

He leaned a little nearer, took her chin between finger and thumb, and turned her face up to the moonlight. "Is your father's name Roger?" he asked.

"Yes," said Polly. "He's in heaven. So is my mamma.

Would you like to come in? The front door is locked, and Aunt Dorcas and Aunt Constantia have taken the key to bed with them, but you can get through the window."

He was a thin man, and nimble, and found that he could. The door was open into the hall and through it he could see the candles on the hall table, lit as though in worship of The Hat. A delightful smile of recognition flashed across his face.

"What have you brought?" asked Polly, trying not to yawn. "Are you the one who brought gold?"

"Yes," he said, and taking out his purse, he opened it that her sleepy eyes might blink at the gleaming sovereigns inside, then closed it and laid it on the little table beside the sofa. "Yes. It would sweeten it, I thought, to bring it home. Oughtn't a little lass of your age to be in bed?"

"Who will let the others in?" asked Polly.

"What others?" he asked.

"Two more," said Polly, yawning outright.

"If anyone else comes with the right to enter I'll let them in," he said and picked her up in his arms. Later on she remembered as though it had been a dream the noiseless way he carried her upstairs and tucked her into her bed with Tibby.

Six

H<small>E WENT BACK</small> to the parlor and stretched himself on the sofa, wrapped in his cloak. He lay with his eyes closed, but he was not asleep. Like Dorcas, he was thinking about time. He had been young and now he was old, and the years between had vanished as though they had never been. . . . It even seemed to him that the old sofa had a lump in exactly the same place.

He was roused by the sound of the church clock striking eleven, and by the sight of a man's head and shoulders thrust through the window. He sat up and observed pleasantly, "Sir, I've a pistol in my pocket."

A voice with a foreign intonation replied with equal pleasantness, "So have I, m'sieur."

"Shall I fire first, or will you?" asked Tom.

"M'sieur, I have no ammunition," said the Frenchman. "Permit me first to place this little token of my affection within the child's stocking which I trust is hanging from the mantelpiece."

"My niece Polly Flowerdew hung her stocking at the foot of her bed," said Tom. "Will you entrust your gift to my care?"

"No," said the Frenchman decidedly. "Nor do I leave this window until I have assured myself that you are indeed related to the ladies of the house, and not some thief come to do them harm."

"You're a wise man," said Tom, getting up and coming to the window. "Will you come inside?"

The Frenchman climbed nimbly in through the window while Tom fetched the candles from the hall and set them on the mantelpiece. Tom took a shabby little case from his pocket, opened it, and showed the other the miniature inside. The Frenchman looked at the delicate heart-shaped face and smiled.

"Pollee grown up," he said.

"My mother when young," said Tom. "You're quite right. I am a thief. I stole it before I ran away to sea."

"M'sieur, I am satisfied," said the Frenchman. "May I ask you of your goodness to give this small gift to your niece? She hoped Father Christmas would give her beads."

Tom held out his large brown hand and the candlelight gleamed on the string of blue turquoises and tiny pearls, and on the small silver cross that hung from them. It was a rosary, a beautiful thing, a treasure such as some princess might have used. Tom laid the rosary upon the table beside the purse of gold. "Gold and frankincense," he said. "Will you stay and drink a glass of wine with me?"

The Frenchman bowed and Tom tiptoed into the dining parlor, unlocked the door and, creeping in, found the wineglasses and old decanter where they had always been, beside the silver biscuit box on the chiffonier. He brought the decanter and glasses back to the parlor, put fresh logs on the dying embers of the fire, and pulled the old armchair forward to the warmth. He established his guest there and poured the wine. Then, sipping his own, he began talking easily of countries he had visited, cities he had seen, adventures by land and sea, until the man beside him began to talk too. By the time the clock struck midnight he had told it all. Men are strange, thought Tom, looking at the fire. Now I could not have taken the word of another, even the best friend that I had, that my wife and son were dead. But then, I am slow to accept bad news. This man would be quick to the point of despair.

The last note of midnight struck and in the silence that came after there was the sound as of a crash from the region of the kitchen.

"The cat has knocked the cream over," said the Frenchman.

"The cat is upstairs with Polly," said Tom. He got up and went soft-footed to the kitchen. The

window was firmly latched and there was no one there. He went farther into the larder and saw that the tiny window had been shattered by a blow from a stone, and through it a dirty bony old hand had been thrust and was grasping a hunk of bread. The hand was withdrawn and then appeared again closing upon a sausage. Tom's hand clasped the wrist. There was no cry of fear from the other side of the window but a glorious tumbling sequence of great oaths that delighted Tom with their rage and richness. Also there was something familiar about them. He leaned closer and saw in the moonlight a face that in spite of great age had changed very little with the years.

"Rags-and-Bones!" he exclaimed with joy. "Praise the Lord! Here's Rags-and-Bones still aboveground!"

"But not for long," said Rags-and-Bones cheerfully. "And I'll not go hungry my last Christmas. Nor dry neither."

"No danger of dryness, Rags-and-Bones," said Tom. "You're drunk as a lord. But you're a wise man. Come in by the parlor window and I'll feed you well. There's an apple pie here, Rags-and-Bones, cold roast beef, pickles, and honey. You've got the loaf. Remember me?"

"I knew you'd come back, Tom Flowerdew," said Rags-and-Bones gleefully. "No gettin' rid of a bad penny."

He disappeared and was at the parlor window almost before Tom had time to get back there. The Frenchman helped him in and put him in the armchair while Tom spread the feast, and then with delight they watched him eat.

"Those are Christmas gifts at your elbow, Rags-and-Bones," said Tom. "They are laid there for my sisters and for Polly. Gold and frankincense."

Rags-and-Bones looked at them, nodded his head but made no comment. When he had finished he said "Amen" loudly and wiped his beard upon a tattered rag that might once have been a handkerchief. Then he got up to go. Both Tom and the Frenchman had slipped their hands into their pockets, feeling there for coins for Rags-and-Bones, but when they looked up at him they were touched by a strange awe, and withdrew their hands empty. To offer him even silver seemed an insult, for there was at this moment a strange majesty about the man. Standing there in the mingled candlelight and moonlight, he looked like a skeleton, but there was regality in his long lean height and the wisdom of the ages in his snowy beard and deep-set eyes. He looked down at the purse and the beads and touched the table beside him with two bony fingers. "Nothing," he said. "Nothing. Yet let the ladies wait. In heaven dead men are alive again and poor men become rich."

Then he was gone. In the quiet night they could

faintly hear his wooden leg stumping along down the deserted street.

"I don't believe I'll see him again," said Tom.

"When he put his fingers on the table Balthasar left myrrh," said the Frenchman. "His death, you understand, to enrich their life."

Seven

ONE WOULD HAVE thought that the state of the
parlor, crumbs on the carpet, empty glasses on the
mantelpiece, and crockery piled up in the hearth,
would in itself have stirred the tidy soul of Dorcas,
and that after her interview with the seafaring man
who had eyed the silver with such interest, Constantia would have been nervously alert. Yet neither
was disturbed. Peace weighed upon the house and
they were wrapped in deep and dreamless slumber.
And so was Polly.

She and Tibby did not wake until the dawn shone

through the uncurtained window straight into their eyes. It was only the first light of dawn, faint and mysterious, but it was enough to show Polly the bumpy outlines of her stocking, and in spite of the disappointment of there being no beads she wriggled up out of her blankets and pounced upon it with glee. Back in her warm nest again with Tibby she held it upside down and shook it joyfully.

There were beads! Tom had been up in the night

and the first thing that fell out was the shining string of pearls and turquoises. It was sad that only Tibby was there to see her rapture, for it was sweet to see. She laughed and sang under her breath and rocked herself with joy. She kissed the beads and held them against her cheek, and at last she hung them around her neck. Then she politely saluted all the other treasures, the sugar mouse, the red ribbon, the apple and the three golden walnuts, the doll, the shell, the pincushion, and the unexpected gift of a netted purse with sixpence inside.

The light strengthened and Polly became aware that there was something unusual about this dawn. All the colors of the rainbow seemed in the sky. She shot out of bed and ran to the window. The sun had not risen yet above the sea but the brown brink of the dawn sky touched it and was mirrored in it, and above it the colors passed through amber and crocus color to palest green, and then to hyacinth blue scattered over with rosy clouds, and these colors too were mirrored in the sea. The morning star still shone, and when Polly opened the window the air was crisp and cool. As she leaned out, breathing in its freshness, all the cocks began to crow. And then her lips parted and the tingling blood sent a glow of warmth to her very fingertips. She leaned out farther, her eyes wide, for three ships were sailing toward the harbor. One had a red sail, and one had a brown sail, and one had a sail like the wing of a swan.

Polly was dressed in the twinkling of an eye, and grabbing her cloak, she sped down the stairs into the parlor. As it was Christmas, when anything unlikely might occur, she was not at all surprised to see that her friend the wise mad Frenchman had joined the first wise man and that both were fast asleep there; one on the sofa with his feet on Aunt Dorcas' best brocade cushion and

the other in the best armchair with his feet on the mantelpiece. She shook them and told them that it was Christmas day in the morning and that three ships were sailing in. She shook them until at last the news penetrated and she had them out in the street and stumbling at her heels as she ran down the hill, with her red cloak streaming out behind her and the bright beads that hung around her neck catching the morning light as they swung to and fro.

They came to the harbor just as the ships entered it, letting down their sails and coming in gently. The two men and Polly ran down the jetty and stood waiting with beating hearts while the three ships glided over the water before them with all composure and all peace. Fishermen manned them but upon the deck of the third ship there stood a lady in a blue cloak and a little child with a golden head. They came a little nearer and they could see the lady's face and suddenly the mad Frenchman gave a great cry, a cry so loud and wild that it seemed to tear the flowery sky into fragments and bring the whole bright dawn tumbling about them in confusion. Then he leaped from the harbor wall to the deck of the third ship, and Polly jumped into her uncle's arms and hid her face against his shoulder and did not see what happened. When she lifted her face again she found that the sun had risen and all the bells of the town were ringing. They made such a noise that she thought all the bells in the world must be ringing, pealing, and clashing over sea and land. The sailors were singing as they made

the boats fast, and Tom was singing and so was she,
and so were all the people in the world.

And all the souls on earth shall sing,
On Christmas day, on Christmas day;
And all the souls on earth shall sing,
On Christmas day in the morning.

Eight

MEANWHILE, in Holly Cottage, Constantia was awake.

"Dorcas, get up!" she cried, shaking her. "I saw three ships!"

"What's that?" asked Dorcas sleepily.

"When I pulled back the curtains I saw three ships in the harbor. Wake up, Dorcas!"

"Three ships?" asked Dorcas, sitting up. "What a fuss about nothing. There are often ships in the harbor." She seemed as usual again. It was Constantia who was lifted out of herself.

"Listen to the bells!" she said. "All the bells on earth!"

"Don't talk nonsense," said Dorcas. "Only our own bells. They always ring on Christmas morning."

"Not like this," said Constantia. "Get up, Dorcas. Polly is not in the house. I have been downstairs and during the night there have been men in the parlor. It smells of tobacco and sherry wine. Your best brocade cushion is crumpled to pieces. There is crockery in the hearth and a purse of gold on the table."

That roused Dorcas. She was out of bed in a flash and in five minutes she and Constantia were dressed. They were just wrenching the curlers from their hair when they heard the running feet in Fish Street. "Put

on your cloak and bonnet, Constantia," said Dorcas. She had dressed herself by the window, where she could keep her eyes on the ships. They were only three fishing boats but their beauty, reflected in the calm water of the harbor, was very great. Who had come sailing in at dawn when the cocks were crowing? The bells clashed out and still the feet in the street were running.

"Come quickly, Constantia," she said. "Bring the key of the front door and come quickly."

She spared only a glance at the state of the parlor as they let themselves out into the bright sunshine of Fish Street. The bells pealed more joyously than

ever and people were running
down the hill. There were lots of
children and they were all laughing.

"What is it?" cried Constantia of a boy who was
running by.

"A little child and his mother have landed," said
the boy.

"Who are they?' cried Dorcas.

"The mad Frenchman knelt on the deck of the ship and kissed the hem of her skirt," answered another voice.

And a third voice cried out, "Tom Flowerdew's come home."

Dorcas and Constantia began to run.

Fish Street had a twist in it, and as they ran around the corner, they saw them coming up the hill. The beautiful woman in her blue cloak was holding the golden-haired little boy by the hand, and he was smiling at the sight of the running feet and the laughing children. With them came two tall men, and for a moment Constantia thought there were three, but when she looked again there were only two. Behind them the sea and the sky were sparklingly blue and gold. The feet of the running children seemed to be dancing to a tune.

> *Then let us all rejoice amain,*
> *On Christmas day, on Christmas day;*
> *Then let us all rejoice amain,*
> *On Christmas day in the morning.*

I Saw Three Ships

lightly & rhythmically
♩ = 100

trad. English
arr. Marshall Brown

I.

I saw three ships come sailing in,
On Christmas day, on Christmas day;
I saw three ships come sailing in,
On Christmas day in the morning.

II.

And what was in those ships all three,
On Christmas day, on Christmas day;
And what was in those ships all three,
On Christmas day in the morning?

III.

The Virgin Mary and Christ were there,
On Christmas day, on Christmas day;
The Virgin Mary and Christ were there,
On Christmas day in the morning.

IV.

Pray, whither sailed those ships all three,
On Christmas day, on Christmas day;
Pray, whither sailed those ships all three,
On Christmas day in the morning?

V.

O they sailed into Bethlehem,
On Christmas day, on Christmas day;
O they sailed into Bethlehem,
On Christmas day in the morning.